Mary

The unwary Sugar-Plum Fairy

A bedtime story and colouring book

By

The Rickety Rhymer

(a decrepit old-timer)

The Rickety Rhymer of Bareham Hall

Is extremely wide and not very tall.

When he walks his body is shaking

His knees crackle, his legs are aching

But still, he manages to raise a smile

Because children's laughter is so worthwhile.

Mary the unwary Sugar-Plum Fairy

Where trickling streams fall to make a distant fountain

And Walter the Mole pushes up a new mountain

As Mandrake the Grass Snake slithers silently by,

A dreamy rainbow lights up a cloudless blue sky

This my friends is Never-never Land,

Where all nasty badness is totally banned.

Here lives a fairy with long purple locks,

Who wears a pink dress and matching socks,

With wings that shimmer like the stars and the sun,

She enjoys helping others while having great fun.

Well, that's Mary, the unwary sugar-plum fairy!

She is a lady so small and so sweet,

Who'd stop at nothing to give folks a treat.

Yet she was really accident prone,

Her whole life being a danger zone.

Poor Mary, the unwary sugar-plum fairy.

She would fly through the land without any fear,

Spreading around her kindness and cheer.

Spells for everything from granting wishes,

To helping with tasks like washing dishes.

Ooh Mary the unwary sugar-plum fairy.

She could decorate a dismal room,

And brighten up the winter gloom.

Add in the glow of a warming fire,

Maybe a settee on which to retire.

Hovering over a kitchen table,

Creating nice food, she was more than able.

Some beans, and egg, and sausage, and chips.

Still not seeing the cat licking its lips.

Good Mary the unwary sugar-plum fairy.

Then the cat leapt up eyes wide with delight,

A flurry of wings, Mary screamed with fright,

She just escaped Cats sharp clawed paw,

Quickly flying out the open door.

Poor Mary the unwary sugar-plum fairy...

She flew over a golf course one hot sunny day,

Hoping to stop the ball from going astray.

But as she flew towards the green,

Somebody's tee shot just wasn't seen,

Lifting her wand to cast her spell,

The star on top was smashed to...H .. well, bits

Down she spiralled out of control,

But the ball bounced twice then into the hole.

Oooh Mary the unwary sugar-plum fairy.

Another day she met a wicked wizard,

He had created a freezing blizzard.

To stop his spell she had to try,

Not wanting snow in mid- July.

She raised her wand and sang a song,

But it all went so very wrong.

The snow all melted, now that was good,

But her home was lost in the following flood.

Poor Mary the unwary sugar-plum fairy.

She met a kind witch one autumn day,

Who said she'd blow Mary's troubles away.

Raising her hands she made a gale,

Leaves left the trees all bald and pale.

Ooh Mary the unwary sugar-plum fairy.

Up in the air Mary spun higher,

Round and around and over a spire.

Then the wind stopped, and she fluttered down,

She felt no change and started to frown

Then Mary felt her powers start to grow,

And her fairy wings began to glow!

Gone are the traumas accident prone brings

Mary dances and Mary sings.

Happy Mary the carefree sugar-plum fairy.

What she did next was very clever

She conjured up her own special weather

Still, plenty of rain but only at night

Sunshine every day, not too hot, just right.

Brilliant Mary sugar-plum fairy.

Now she wanted to help folk even more

She left magical seeds at everyone's door

Without having to work for hours and hours

All their gardens were soon full of flowers

Amazing Mary sugar-plum fairy.

Mary added in some very special beans

That grew all their veggies and all their greens

Plenty of cabbage, carrots, sweet corn and swedes

Always enough to suit everyone's needs

Magical Mary sugar-plum fairy.

Neverland was full of colour and sweet scent

Fairy folk were smiling wherever you went

Mary was a hero all over their world

No longer the unwary fairy girl.

Hero Mary the sugar-plum fairy!

All that knew her felt so much pride

She was well known both far and wide

Something happened that was never planned,

Tales of Mary even reached Lapland

Fair Mary, the carefree sugar-plum fairy.

Santa, in his grotto listening to his elves

Heard of this lady doing deeds like themselves.

She sounded kind, pretty and sweet.

Wouldn't it be nice if they could meet?

Oooh, Mary, the carefree sugar-plum fairy.

Santa rang Mary that very same day,

Asked her to come for a ride on his sleigh.

Over hot deserts, green woods and Atlantic

Their worldwide journey was so romantic,

Joyful Mary, the carefree sugar-plum fairy.

Mile after mile together they flew.

Smile after smile their love just grew.

Santa knew Mary could grant people's wishes,

So, Santa asked Mary to become his Mrs.

She didn't leave him long to guess

She quickly answered Yes, yes, yes

Mary glowed with beaming delight

Her eyes sparkling like the moonlight

Blissful Mary the carefree sugar-plum fairy.

They saw no reason to delay,

They set the date straight away

They chose a quiet church for their marriage.

With reindeer to pull their golden carriage

Delighted Mary, the carefree sugar-plum fairy.

Mary made her dress in finest silk,

A train and a sash all white as milk

Precious jewels encrusted her gown.

And on her head a shimmering crown.

Sparkling Mary our sugar-plum fairy

All the elves formed the guard of honour,

Mary felt the joy of love bestowed upon her.

The vicar heard them say their vows

Our Mary lives very happily now.

Now you all know what came to pass.

Mary, our sugar-plum fairy, becomes Mary Christmas.

Mary Our Beautiful Bride

Welcome Home Mary

Where trickling streams fall to make a distant fountain

And Walter the Mole pushes up a new mountain

As Mandrake the Grass Snake slithers silently by,

A dreamy rainbow lights up the cloudless blue sky

There in a wooded dell in Never-Never Land

There's a huge celebration being planned

In a silky web tent, the spiders have made

A buffet of gorgeous food has been laid.

Lots of ice cream, cake and glasses of Fanta-

All because Mary has married our Santa.

The fairy toadstool homes, they form a wide ring

Where fairies, elves and pixies can all dance and sing.

After the planning, Mary's friend, Isobella Faye,

Is looking out for Santa and his reindeer sleigh

Bringing back our Mary for her special do

It's all a big secret; they just don't have a clue

Bells start jingling as the sleigh comes in to land,

Then the welcoming sound of a pixie jazz band.

The reindeer have landed amid loud applause

And all are excited to see who's on board.

Mary waved and smiled to all her friends,

Overjoyed, to share their company again.

Isobella bowed low, then shook Santa's hand,

A special greeting to their fairy homeland.

Will o' the wisp lamps light up the silk tent,

A million rose petals add a fragrant scent.

The pixie jazz music soon had them all swinging,

Fairies all a flurry and sweet voices singing.

All were invited to join the fun and the dancing-

Even the reindeer enjoyed their clumsy prancing.

Round and around, they danced all through the night.

Nobody left until the first golden sunlight

Broke through the darkness on the fairy nation,

Lighting up the closing of their celebration.

Now it was time for Santa and Mary to fly,

Everybody hugged them, said thanks and goodbye.

Wrapped in warm blankets for their morning flight,

They were a little tired but smiled with delight.

Going back to Lapland for their new life together,

Where they'll be granting folks' wishes for ever and ever.

*****

Thank You for buying my little book.